Rusty

Saddle Up Series
Book 52

Dave and Pat Sargent are longtime residents of Prairie Grove, Arkansas. Dave, a fourth-generation dairy farmer, began writing in early December 1990. Pat, a former teacher, began writing shortly after. They enjoy the outdoors and have a real love for animals.

Rusty

Saddle Up Series
Book 52

By Dave and Pat Sargent

Beyond "The End"
By Sue Rogers

Illustrated by Jane Lenoir

Ozark Publishing, Inc.
P.O. Box 228
Prairie Grove, AR 72753

Cataloging-in-Publication Data

Sargent, Dave, 1941–
  Rusty / by Dave and Pat Sargent ; illustrated
by Jane Lenoir.—Prairie Grove, AR :
Ozark Publishing, c2004.
      p. cm. (Saddle up series ; 52)

    "Be strong and brave"—Cover.
    SUMMARY: At the Rocking S Horse
Ranch, a wild red roan named Rusty
declares that no one will become his boss.
But when a cowboy named Slim breaks him,
they decide to work together to demonstrate
that no one else can ride Rusty. Includes
factual information about red roan horses.
    ISBN 1-56763-803-1 (hc)
           1-56763-804-X (pbk)

    1. Horses—Juvenile fiction. [1. Horses—
Fiction. 2. Cowboys-—Fiction. 3. Rodeos—
Fiction.] I. Sargent, Pat, 1936– II. Lenoir,
Jane, 1950– ill. III. Title. IV. Series.

    PZ7.S2465Ru 2004
    [Fic]—dc21   2001007599

Printed in the United States of America

Inspired by

red roans that are a light color in the spring and get darker each season.

Dedicated to

all children with hair that changes color with the sun.

Foreword

Rusty is a wild red roan who was rounded up one day by cowboys from the Rocking S Horse Ranch. When the wild horses were counted, each cowboy knew that he'd have four horses to break.

"Break!" neighed the red roan. "What does that mean?"

Saddle-up! It's *rodeo* time!

Contents

If you would like to have the authors of the Saddle Up Series visit your school, free of charge, call 1-800-321-5671 or 1-800-960-3876.

One

Wild Horses!

The roar of thundering hooves echoed across the vast countryside. Horses of all sizes and colors raced ahead of ten cowboys who were chasing them toward the corral at the Rocking S Horse Ranch. Rusty the red roan and a dapple grey led the herd with their heads held high.

"I have a feeling that something exciting is about to happen," Rusty nickered.

"Humph!" the dapple grey said with a snort. "And just what gives you that idea? I was really looking forward to grazing and roaming the hills with our friends. I would not call this exciting."

As they approached the open gate, Rusty put his head down and snorted before cautiously trotting into the corral. Moments later, he and the rest of the herd were circling the fenced enclosure as the cowboys quickly shut the gate behind them.

"We have them captured now," the ranch foreman yelled. "Each of you hands pick out the horse you want to start breaking."

Rusty skidded to a halt and glared at the man in the gray Stetson hat.

"Just what do you mean by 'break'?" he neighed. "No man will ever break me. I am my own boss!"

"I want that red roan," a slow-talking cowboy said quietly.

The other cowboys laughed, and the ranch foreman said, "That one's a renegade, Slim. Maybe you should start with that linebacked dun or that silver grullo over there."

"Nope," Slim replied, looking at Rusty. "That's the horse for me."

Rusty Red Roan put his ears forward and stared at the tall cowboy before shaking his head.

"I think I could like you," he said. "But I am my own boss."

The ranch foreman chuckled and said, "Each of you cowhands will be breaking four horses apiece. You better get to work."

The cowboys started swinging their ropes as the horses trotted past them in the corral.

One by one, large loops sailed through the air and settled over the heads of passing horses.

A short time later, saddles were tossed on the backs of the roped horses. As the first cowboy swung onto the back of the white horse, the first bronc ride started.

"Get off my back!" the white horse snorted. He lowered his head and began bucking. His hind hooves flew high in the air, and the cowboys began clapping and yelling.

"Keep your seat on the saddle, Clyde!"

"Don't let that little ole white horse throw you," another laughed.

Two minutes later, the bucking and squealing was still going on. Rusty stayed close by, urging the white to throw the cowboy off.

Suddenly, the white stopped bucking. The cowboy tipped his hat toward the men who were standing there, laughing and clapping.

"One down," the cowboy said with a smile. "Three to go."

"Humph," the red roan snorted. "I'll never give up that easily."

For three hours, the red roan watched his friends buck and run and rear, trying to throw their riders on the ground. But in the end, each one settled down and accepted its role as a saddle horse. Rusty noticed Slim looking at him several times, but he kept tossing his loop over another horse's head.

"When are you going to ride that red roan?" the ranch foreman finally asked.

"Right now," Slim answered with a grin. "I was just saving the best for last."

"Better let me try him first, Slim," one of the cowboys sneered.

"I don't think you are rider enough to handle him."

Rusty snorted and shook his head.

"I don't like that fellow, Slim," he muttered. "Nobody's going to be my boss, especially not him."

Slim looked at the red roan and smiled, then said quietly, "Go ahead, Roy. Give him a try. After you get thrown, I'll show you how to be a real cowboy."

Minutes later, the red roan felt a saddle on his back for the first time. Slim talked softly to him as Roy got set to mount. Then the soft-spoken cowboy stepped out of the way.

For a brief moment, Rusty did not move. Then Roy kicked him with the heels of his boots. The red roan sprang high into the air.

"Get off me!" he snorted. I am my own boss!" And with the second leap, Roy sailed off Rusty's back. As he hit the ground with a thud, all of the horses laughed.

"That's the way to go, Rusty," the palomino nickered. "He's not a nice man."

Rusty held his head high as he trotted around the fallen cowboy.

"I want another try at him," Roy complained. "No horse is going to make a fool out of me."

"Really?" Rusty said with a snort. "Well, come on, cowboy. Let's go another round."

Two

The One-Man Horse

The sun was overhead when Roy hit the dirt for the third time.

"Come on, Roy. This is fun! Don't quit now," Rusty nickered. "I'm ready for a fourth round."

Slim quietly walked up to the red roan and stroked his nose with one hand. The red roan sighed and murmured, "You seem to be nice." Then he jerked his head around and glared at the man who was sprawled on the ground. "But I don't like your attitude, mister!"

Roy hobbled out of the corral. Slim said, "Okay, Rusty. Roy had his turn. He tried three times. Now, it's my turn. I'm going to ride you."

"I don't think so," the red roan said quietly. "We'll see."

Slim was on his back with his feet in the stirrups before the red roan realized what had happened. He liked this fellow, but...

"I am my own boss!" Rusty neighed as he reared high up on his hind legs. As his front hooves came back down onto the ground, his head went down, and his hind legs went up. He bucked back and forth across the corral like a coiled spring, but Slim did not leave his back.

"You are one good cowboy, Slim," Rusty snorted. But I keep telling you that I am my own boss."

Minutes passed as the horse and rider traveled up and down and back and forth across the corral.

The ranch foreman and the other cowboys stood in stunned silence as the red roan used every trick to remove the rider from his back. Finally Rusty came to a halt. He was breathing heavily, and his neck was lathered.

"Okay, Boss," Rusty gasped. "You win."

He looked around at the man on his back and added, "But you are the only one I will allow on me."

That evening Slim walked to the corral with a small bucket of oats. He set it in front of Rusty then began gently stroking his neck.

"You are a fine horse, Rusty," he said. "I want to buy you, but I don't have enough money."

Rusty took a big bite of the oats before nodding his head.

"I would like for you to be my boss," he murmured. "We make a good team."

Slim stroked the red roan's nose and said, "Don't worry, my friend. I'll think of some way to own you."

The following morning several cowboys were lined up in the corral. Each one wanted to ride Rusty Roan.

"Slim is wanting to buy him," the ranch foreman explained, "but he is short of the amount of money that he needs."

Slim looked at the red roan and winked.

"Tell you what, boys," he said with a chuckle. "I'm not a betting man, but if this red roan throws you before eight seconds pass, you can

donate five dollars to my black hat."
He took off his hat and placed it
upside down on a gatepost. "I think
Rusty is a one-man horse."

"There's no such thing as a one-man horse, Slim. You got yourself a deal," one of the cowboys laughed. The other cowboys agreed.

Roy glared at the red roan as he rubbed a sore shoulder. "You broke him yesterday. I'm ready to try my luck again today," he said as he reached into his pocket. He took out a five-dollar bill, placed it in Slim's hat, and walked over to Rusty.

The red roan nodded his head at Slim as Roy jumped into the saddle.

"I can handle this one, Boss," he nickered. "Get ready for one wild and crazy bronc ride!"

Three

It's Rodeo Time!

Cowhands sat along the fence, watching the red roan as Roy's boot heels hit him in the sides. Rusty did not move. Roy kicked him again, but the red roan just stood there. He acted like he didn't know there was a man on his back. The cowhands started laughing and pointing at the horse and rider.

"Better get your five dollars ready," Roy sneered as he leaned back in the saddle. "You just lost. Look, I'm still on him."

Then Rusty lowered his head to the ground. At the same moment, his hind legs soared high the air. Roy was airborne for ten seconds before finally hitting the ground.

"Ouch!" Rusty muttered as he watched the cowboy crawl toward the fence. "That probably hurt."

He looked at Slim and asked with a nod, "How was that, Boss?" Slim face had a big smile on it.

Slim winked at him then turned toward the other cowboys.

"Okay, who wants to try riding Rusty Red Roan next?" he asked.

Throughout the long afternoon Rusty bucked and reared and turned in little circles. He tried a new trick with each cowboy, and every trick worked. As the last cowhand hit the dirt, the foreman shook Slim's hand.

Slim walked over and took his hat off the gatepost. It was full of five-dollar bills. He handed the bills to the foreman and said, "Here's the money for Rusty."

"Congratulations," the foreman said. "You are now the proud owner of the feisty red roan."

Slim smiled and walked over to the red roan. Rusty was very happy. A big tear trickled down his face.

Late that night, the red roan heard a noise. He felt good when Slim quietly entered his stall.

"Howdy, Boss," he nickered. "What are you doing up so late?"

Slim sat down on a bale of hay and said, "Rusty, I couldn't sleep. I've been thinking that you and I can make more money in bronc riding than we can in cowboying. What do you think about the idea?"

The red roan nodded his head and gently nuzzled Slim on the cheek.

"You and I can travel through the west and see some new country," Slim continued. "And when we run short of money, we'll find some eager cowboys who think they're good enough riders to stay on you."

"Sounds like fun, Boss!" Rusty said. "Let's go."

Three weeks later, the red roan and his new boss Slim trotted into the town of Limon, Colorado. News of the powerful one-man bronc had traveled fast from the cowhands on the Rocking S Horse Ranch. Within a short time, cowboys were lined up along the street to give Slim their five dollars for the chance to ride Rusty Red Roan. Each rider felt that he would win the money.

As the sun peeked over the eastern horizon the next morning, Slim rode Rusty into a big round corral.

"Last night I was visiting with some of the local cowboys," Slim said quietly. "They want to have a roping contest, too. It sounds like a good idea to me. It would give the guys a chance to compete against one another and win some money. They want us to set it up."

"Sounds good to me, Boss," Rusty nickered. "I can outrun any calf they have, if you can rope it."

Slim reined Rusty to a halt in the center of the corral. "You know, Rusty," he said, "I think this bronc-riding and calf-roping thing could become a real popular sport."

"Hmmm," Rusty was thinking. "It's possible that bronc riding and calf roping could be entertaining for folks. But what could we call it?"

"Maybe we could call this sport the *Big Ride*," he said. "Or maybe we could call it *Rode*. I've got it, Boss! We can call it **Rodeo**!"

"Hmmm. Tell me something, Rusty. What do you think of the name **Rodeo**?" Slim asked.

Rusty quickly nodded his head.

People from far and near who had read the posters had gathered around. They had to pay to enter the rodeo, and they had to pay to watch.

When the first cowboy mounted Rusty, the red roan began twisting and turning and then tossed him high in the air. The crowd went wild!

"Hmmm," Rusty thought. "My boss has started a sport called *rodeo*. Folks will enjoy it for years to come, but I just wonder if they'll remember Boss Slim and his red roan rodeo horse named Rusty."

As he tossed his rider high into the air, he nickered, "Ah, who cares? Life is wonderful and just getting better and better! Come on, all you cowboys, let's rodeo!"

Four

Red Roan Facts

Cowboys call a bay roan a red roan. Horses with this roan pattern will usually have small dark spots, not caused by scars. A branding iron could possibly leave this look. As the horses age, the spots increase.

To cowboys, a roan has a mix of colored and white hairs, but *roan* describes one pattern in horses.

Red roans are light in the spring. In the summer, they are brownish. They are darkest in the winter and do not look like a roan.

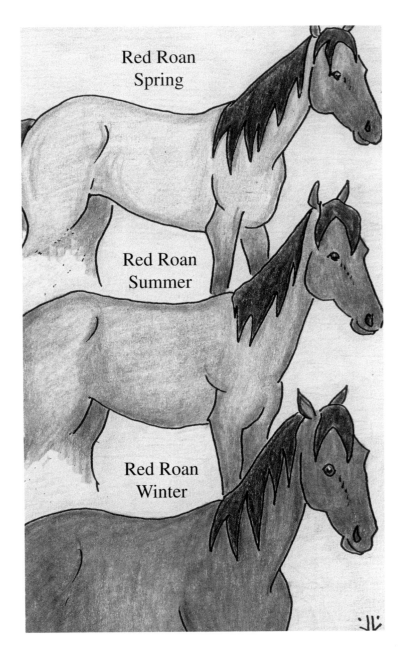

Red Roan
Spring

Red Roan
Summer

Red Roan
Winter

BEYOND "THE END"

A horse doesn't care how much you know
until he knows how much you care.
Pat Parell

WORD LIST
red roan
nicker
trot
rope
nuzzle
hoof
bronc riding
dapple grey
snort
saddle
calf roping
linebacked dun
canter
loop

hock
silver grullo
neigh
neck
stirrups
muzzle
fetlock
palomino

From the word list above, write:

1. One word that tells how a horse shows affection.
2. Two words that name rodeo events.
3. Two words that tell gaits of a horse.
4. Three words for sounds horses make.
5. Four words that name tack for a horse.
6. Five words that name points on a horse.
7. Five words that describe colors of horses.
What color are manes and tails of palomino horses?

CURRICULUM CONNECTIONS

A red roan is a mixture of white and brown hairs with black mane, tail, and stockings. What color is your hair?

Genes determine the color of a horse just as genes determine the color of your hair.

Take a survey of the color of hair for everyone in the classroom. Write Blond, Brown, Red, and Black on the chalkboard. Record the survey results, making a graph of hair color. Which color hair has the most names; which color hair has the least names?

Examine a strand of hair under a microscope. Look at a hair from a horse, if available. Compare the two.

Describe a bronc-riding event. Describe a calf-roping event. Have you been to a rodeo? Slim and Rusty began the first rodeo in Limon, Colorado. Find Colorado on a globe. Are there rodeos in your state?

Find your state on the globe. How far is your state from Colorado?

PROJECT

Combine your math and artistic skills! Draw to scale and accurately color a picture (body, tail, and mane) of the horse that is featured in each book read in the Saddle Up Series. You could soon have sixty horses prancing around the walls of your classroom!

Learning + horses = FUN.

Look in your school library media center for books about how to draw a horse and the colors of horses. Don't forget the useful information in the last chapter of this book (Red Roan Facts) and the picture on the book cover for a shape and color guide.

HELPFUL HINTS AND WEBSITES
A horse is measured in hands. One hand equals four inches. Use a scale of 1" equals 1 hand.

41

Visit website <www.equisearch.com> to find a glossary of equine terms, information about tack and equipment, breeds, art and graphics, and more about horses. Learn more at <www.horse-country.com> and at <www.ansi.okstate.edu/breeds/horses/>.

KidsClick! is a web search for kids by librarians. There are many interesting websites here. HORSES and HORSEMANSHIP are two of the more than 600 subjects. Visit <www.kidsclick.org>.

Is your classroom beginning to look like the Rocking S Horse Ranch? Happy Trails to You!